Dear Parents:

Congratulations! Your child is taking the first steps on an exciting journey. The destination? Independent reading!

STEP INTO READING® will help your child get there. The program offers five steps to reading success. Each step includes fun stories and colorful art or photographs. In addition to original fiction and books with favorite characters, there are Step into Reading Non-Fiction Readers, Phonics Readers and Boxed Sets, Sticker Readers, and Comic Readers—a complete literacy program with something to interest every child.

Learning to Read, Step by Step!

Ready to Read Preschool–Kindergarten
• big type and easy words • rhyme and rhythm • picture clues
For children who know the alphabet and are eager to begin reading.

Reading with Help Preschool–Grade 1
• basic vocabulary • short sentences • simple stories
For children who recognize familiar words and sound out new words with help.

Reading on Your Own Grades 1–3
• engaging characters • easy-to-follow plots • popular topics
For children who are ready to read on their own.

Reading Paragraphs Grades 2–3
• challenging vocabulary • short paragraphs • exciting stories
For newly independent readers who read simple sentences with confidence.

Ready for Chapters Grades 2–4
• chapters • longer paragraphs • full-color art
For children who want to take the plunge into chapter books but still like colorful pictures.

STEP INTO READING® is designed to give every child a successful reading experience. The grade levels are only guides; children will progress through the steps at their own speed, developing confidence in their reading.

Remember, a lifetime love of reading starts with a single step!

Visit us on the Web!
StepIntoReading.com
randomhousekids.com

Educators and librarians, for a variety of teaching tools, visit us at RHTeachersLibrarians.com

ISBN 978-1-5247-2068-1 (trade) — ISBN 978-1-5247-2069-8 (lib. bdg.)

Printed in the United States of America

10 9 8 7 6 5 4 3 2

Random House Children's Books supports the First Amendment and celebrates the right to read.

STEP INTO READING®

RUSTY RIVETS

Magnet Power!

by Tex Huntley

based on the teleplay
"Rusty Digs In" by Ravi Steve

illustrated by Donald Cassity

Random House New York

Today is an important day for Rusty.

His friend Mr. Higgins
will get a medal!
Mr. Higgins is the
town's first inventor.

Rusty made the medal.

It is gold and shiny.

Oh, no!

The medal is missing.

Rusty thinks

Botasaur buried it.

How can Rusty and Ruby
check all the holes
in the yard?

Maybe Rusty's
really powerful magnet
can find the medal.

The magnet finds cans,
plane wings, and even Jack.
It does not find the medal.
Botasaur did not bury it.

Rusty puts
a metal detector
on Ruby's buggy.

Now they can search

all over town.

Time to bolt!

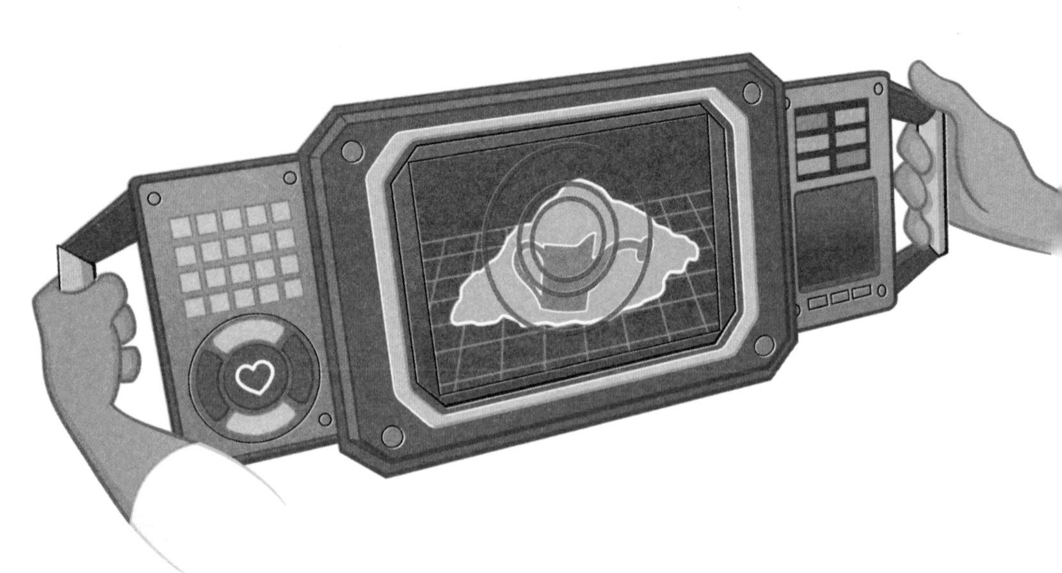

Beep. Beep. Beep.

The metal detector

does not find the medal.

A seagull flies overhead.

Beep. Beep. BEEP!

The seagull has the medal!

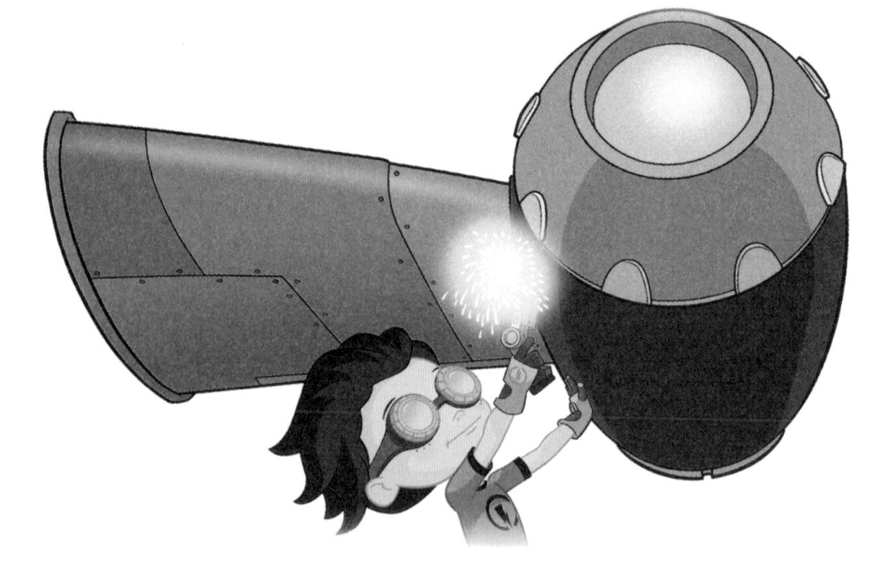

Let's combine it
and design it!
Rusty puts the magnet and
plane wings on Botasaur.

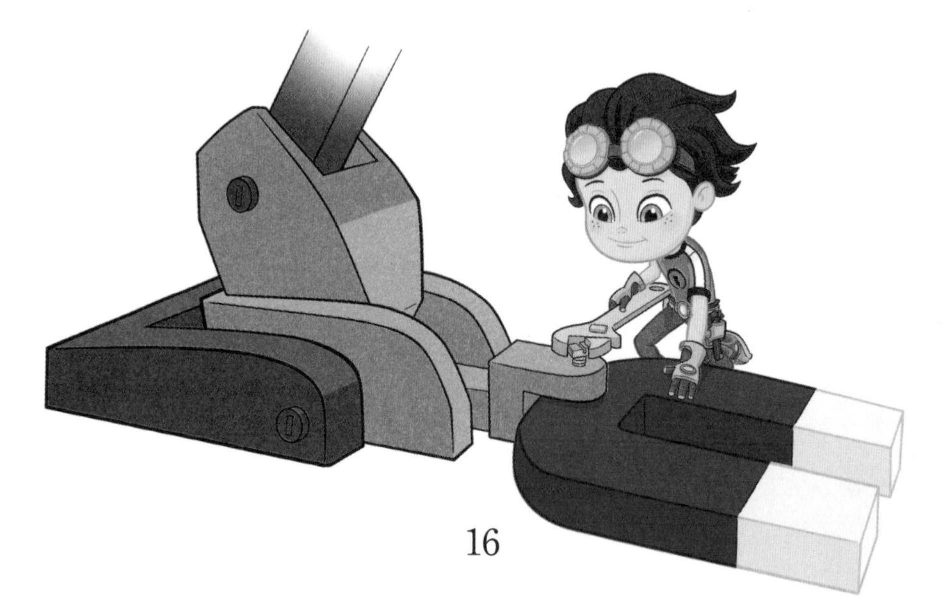

Rusty and Botasaur

take off!

Rusty and Botasaur
go after the seagull.
They fly higher
and higher.

Botasaur gets the medal with the magnet.

Botasaur and Rusty
reach the stage
just in time!

Ranger Anna gives
Mr. Higgins the medal.
Hooray for Mr. Higgins!

Botasaur is a hero!

Rusty makes a really big medal for him.

Botasaur buries

his medal!

Hooray for Botasaur!

THE USBORNE BOOK OF PREHISTORIC FACTS

Annabel Craig

CONTENTS

Illustrated by Tony Gibson
Additional illustrations by Ian Jackson, Kevin Maddison and Rod Sutterby

Designed by Tony Gibson
Additional designs by Joe Coonan and Stephen Meir

Researched by William Lindsay, British Museum (Natural History)
Additional research by Frances Paget

What is prehistory?

Going back in time

History is the story of human beings that is learned from written records: it goes back about 5,500 years to the first known writing.

Prehistory is anything older than that; it is the story of life on Earth that is learnt from fossils. It begins about 3,500 million years ago with the first known living things.

In this book, m.y.a. stands for 'million years ago'.

Earth's time chart

This time chart shows Earth's history, counting each year as one second since the Earth was formed, 4,600 m.y.a.

Formation of the Earth	146 years ago
Earliest known living cells	100 years ago
Jellyfish, worms, sponges	18 years ago
Early reptiles	10 years ago
Dinosaurs, early mammals	6 years ago
First apes	1 year ago
Modern human beings	11 hours ago
Beginning of civilisation	2¾ hours ago
Egyptian pyramids built	1¼ hours ago
Birth of Jesus Christ	33 minutes ago
Columbus discovered America	8 minutes ago
Men landed on the Moon	17 seconds ago

DID YOU KNOW?

In 1656, James Ussher, an Irish Archbishop, calculated from the Bible that the Earth was created at 8 pm. on Saturday, 3 October, 4004 BC. Although some people believe that scientists' ideas of evolution are wrong, not many people believe in Ussher's date.

Measuring time

There are several different calendars for counting years. Most of the western world uses the calendar which starts from the birth of Jesus Christ. Chinese, Muslim

and Jewish calendars have different starting dates. Calendars can be used to give exact dates in history. The dates for years in prehistory are not exact because no one really knows them; but they give the order in which events are thought to have happened.

How do we know?

Fossil facts

Fossils are the remains of plants or animals, which have, over millions of years, been turned into stone. By studying them, and comparing them to living things, it is possible to build a picture of life on Earth long ago. New fossils are always being found, adding to the picture, or changing it. Any information we have about prehistory comes from fossils.

A variety of fossils

Most fossils found are of the hard parts of plants and animals. A few are of tracks or prints they made.
They can be:
bones
shells
teeth
horns
skin
hair
footprints
leafprints
eggs
droppings

Carbon 14 dating

Radioactive carbon rays are absorbed by living things. After death, the rays decay at a steady rate. By counting these rays, it is possible to date fossils up to 100,000 years old.

living person	2,500 rays per hour
5,600 year old skull	1,250 rays per hour
11,200 year old skull	625 rays per hour
44,000 year old skull	3 rays per hour

A small chance

The chance of anything becoming a fossil is very small. It must be buried rapidly after death. Over thousands or millions of years, it hardens into stone and is buried

under layers of rock. The chance of a fossil being found are also small. The rock in which it lies must be raised to the surface (by movements of the Earth's surface). Wind and rain must then wear the rock away to expose it. The fossil must be discovered soon after that before it is worn away.

How old is it?

Rocks lie in layers and if they are not disturbed, the lower layer will be older than the upper layer. A fossil will be as old as the rocks in which it is found. The deepest gorge in the Earth's surface is the Grand Canyon, USA. There 2,000 million years of rock layers and fossil history can be found.

Time tape

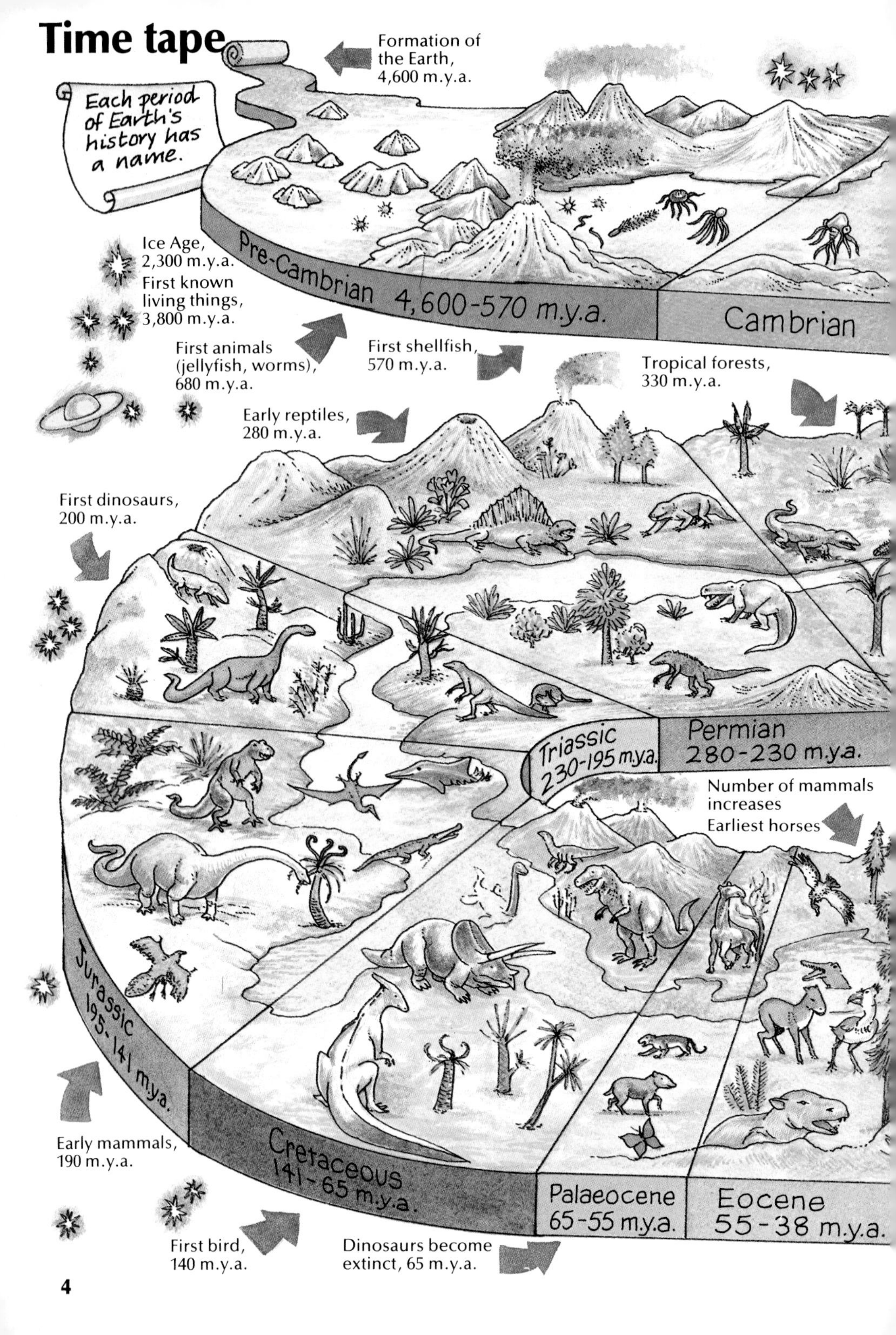

Each period of Earth's history has a name.
Formation of the Earth, 4,600 m.y.a.
Ice Age, 2,300 m.y.a.
First known living things, 3,800 m.y.a.
First animals (jellyfish, worms), 680 m.y.a.
First shellfish, 570 m.y.a.
Pre-Cambrian 4,600-570 m.y.a.
Cambrian
Tropical forests, 330 m.y.a.
Early reptiles, 280 m.y.a.
First dinosaurs, 200 m.y.a.
Triassic 230-195 m.y.a.
Permian 280-230 m.y.a.
Number of mammals increases
Earliest horses
Jurassic 195-141 m.y.a.
Cretaceous 141-65 m.y.a.
Palaeocene 65-55 m.y.a.
Eocene 55-38 m.y.a.
Early mammals, 190 m.y.a.
First bird, 140 m.y.a.
Dinosaurs become extinct, 65 m.y.a.

First fish, 500 m.y.a.
First plants live on land, 400 m.y.a.
570 - 500 m.y.a.
Ordovician 500-435 m.y.a.
First amphibians, 350 m.y.a.
Carboniferous 345-280 m.y.a.
Devonian 395-345 m.y.a.
Silurian 435-395 m.y.a.
Earliest insects, 380 m.y.a.
Earliest apes
Man-apes, 5 m.y.a.
First human beings, 2 m.y.a.
Last Ice Age begins, 2 m.y.a.
First civilisations, 10,000 years ago.
Oligocene 38-22 m.y.a.
Miocene 22-6 m.y.a.
Pliocene 6-2 m.y.a.
Pleistocene 2 m.y.a.- 10,000 years
Holocene 10,000 years ago to present.

The beginning of life

First life on Earth

The first known life on Earth is 3,200 million years old. Fossils of tiny cells were found in cherts (a type of flint) in South Africa. These cells floated in water and were so small that hundreds would have fitted on this full-stop.

Stone blankets

In Zimbabwe, Africa, there are large mounds of limestone called stromatolites ('stone blankets'). They are deposits made by tiny plant cells, called blue-green algae, 3,000 m.y.a. These cells can still be found forming stromatolites in Shark Bay, Australia.

Oxygen is a gas in the air we breathe. It forms a layer, called the ozone layer, high in the atmosphere around the Earth. It protects life on Earth from the Sun's dangerous ultra-violet rays and it makes our sky look blue.

Plants make oxygen

Plants lived long before the first animals. They made oxygen, which animals breathe to stay alive. Until there was enough oxygen, there could be no animal life. Blue-green algae are among the first plants known to have made oxygen. All people and living animals today breathe oxygen made by trees and plants.

The first animals

Fossils of the first known animals were found at Ediacara, Australia. Some are of jellyfish as big as lorry wheels. Fossils of soft-bodied animals are rare, but the shape of these jellyfish, stranded on a beach 670 m.y.a., was preserved by a layer of sand before they rotted.

Amazing But True

Trilobites were the first animals to have eyes. Human beings have one lens in each eye, but some trilobites had as many as 20,000. Over 10,000 species of trilobites are known. They appeared 570 m.y.a. and disappeared 230 m.y.a. They are the ancestors of today's shrimps and lobsters.

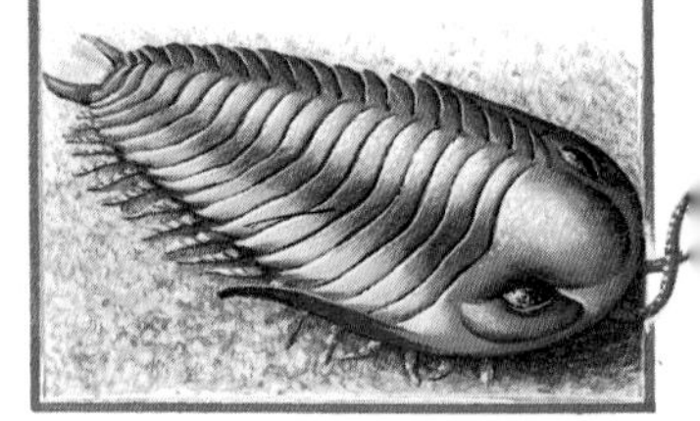

Cambrian

Ordovician

What did *not* exist in the Cambrian Period (570-500 m.y.a.)

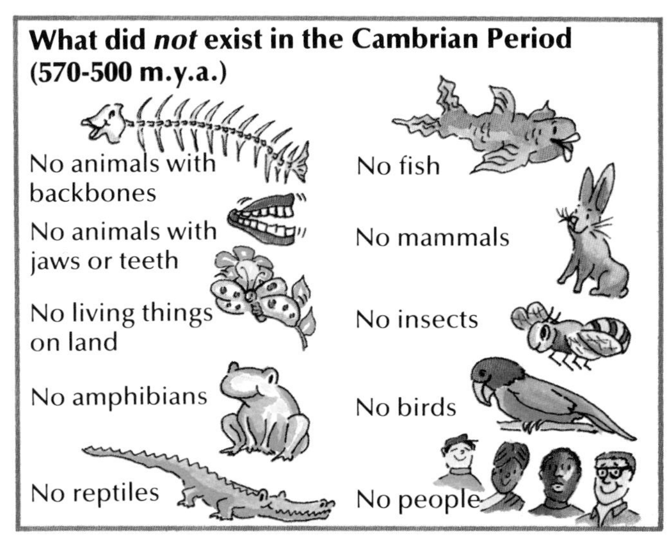

Growing a shell

The first known shellfish lived during the Cambrian Period, 570-500 m.y.a. Growing a shell or skeleton outside the body gave animals protection and an enormous number of new animals developed. Shellfish have the best recorded history of any animal as their shells were easily fossilized.

Submarine gardens

Not all animals look like animals. Crinoids, or sea-lilies, looked like flowers. Along their many arms, they had rows of tubes which collected food from the water.

Most common fossils

Brachiopods (lamp-shells) are the most common fossils found. There are about 300 species living in the seas today; but at least 30,000 different species lived in the past.

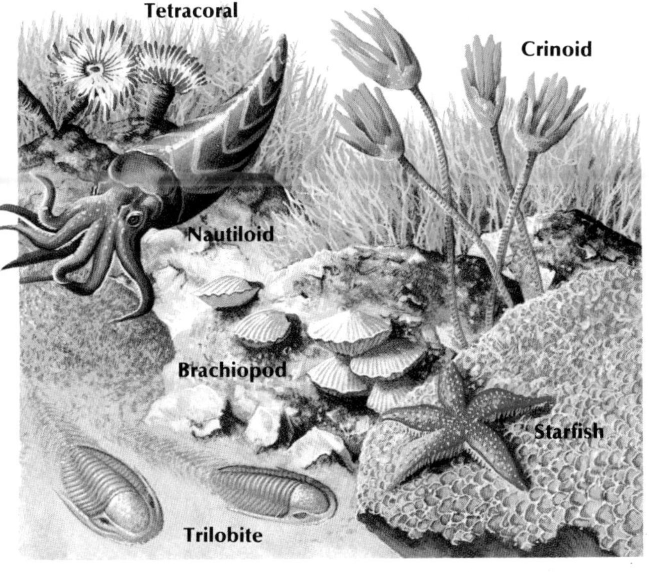

Shells on the move

Nautiloids were shellfish that could swim because their shells contained chambers of gas and water. They floated up or down by emptying or filling the chambers with water, and moved forward by sucking in and squirting out water. Some were cone-shaped and grew to a length of 4.5m (15ft), as long as 40 ice-cream cones.

Creatures of the sea

The first fish

The first vertebrates (animals with a backbone) were the first fish, called Ostracoderms. The name means 'bony skin'. They had no jaws, so they could not grasp or chew food. Instead they sucked in muddy water, filtering out tiny pieces of food.

Jaws

By the Devonian Period, 395 m.y.a., fish called Placoderms had developed jaws. This meant they could eat other fish and had a bigger choice of food. Many new species of fish developed and so the Devonian is known as the 'Age of Fish'.

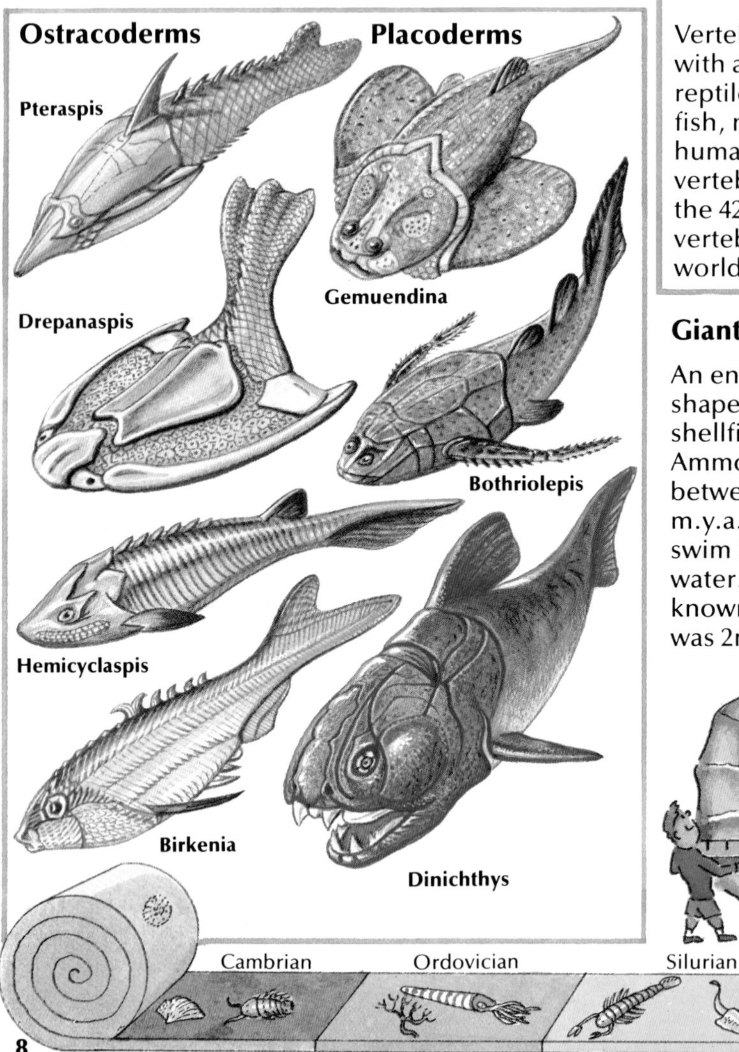

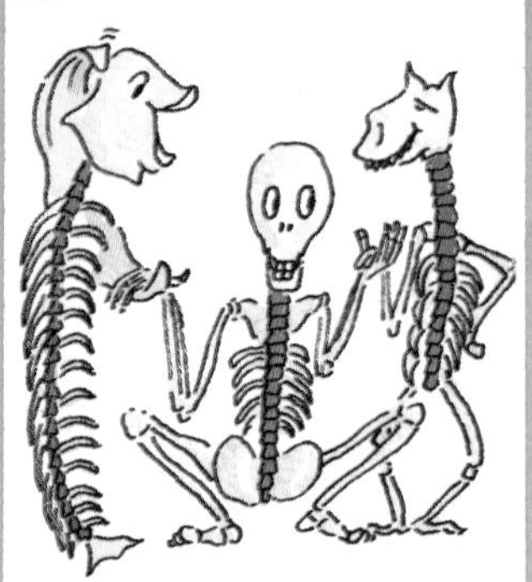

Vertebrates are animals with a backbone. Birds, reptiles, amphibians, fish, mammals (and human beings) are all vertebrates. Over half of the 42,000 species of vertebrates known in the world are fish.

Giant shells

An enormous number of shapes and sizes of shellfish called Ammonites lived between 230 and 65 m.y.a. They were able to swim by pumping out water. The largest known, Parapuzosia, was 2m (6ft) in diameter.

Cambrian Ordovician Silurian Devonian

After millions of years, fish began to grow teeth. Teeth developed out of bony armour near the mouths of armoured fish.

The coral calendar

Today there are 365 days in a year, but 570 m.y.a., there were 428. Scientists know that coral grows a band of skeleton each day, and that it grows more at night than in the daylight. Counting these bands on fossil coral gives the number of days in a year, millions of years ago.

Gigantic jaws

The largest prehistoric fish was Carcharodon megalodon that lived 22 m.y.a. This ancestor of today's great white shark was as long as a lorry. It had teeth the size of a human hand, and could open its jaws so wide that four people could have stood in its mouth.

Monster of the deep

The most ferocious fish in the Devoninan seas was Dinichthys. It was over four times longer than a windsurf board. Its massive armoured head had jaws with sharp biting blades about 60cm (2ft) long.

Fish feet

About 370 m.y.a., there were long periods of hot, dry weather when many rivers and lakes dried up. A fish called Eusthenopteron was able to live out of water because it had a lung as well as gills. It could pull itself across the ground in search of water, using its strong fins which had bones. Eusthenopteron is believed to be the ancestor of amphibians, because its fin bones look like the leg bones of amphibians. Amphibians were the first vertebrates to live on land.

Land invasion

The first land-plant

The first plant known to live on land, called Cooksonia, was found in Wales. It was only the size of short grass, and had no leaves, no roots, and no flowers.

A system of tubes

Plants that live in the sea are surrounded by water which keeps them wet and holds them upright. To live on land, plants needed a waterproof outer layer to stop them drying out. They

developed woody tubes inside to send water through all the stems, and which also stiffened them, acting like a skeleton, so they could stand upright. The first plant to have these tubes (called a vascular plant) was Cooksonia.

The coal forests

The hot, steamy forests of the Carboniferous Period (345-280 m.y.a.) contained these plants which have been identified from their fossils.

Lepidodendron, a gigantic clubmoss

Calamites, a giant horsetail

Psaronius, a tree fern

Medullosa, a seed fern

Small horsetail

30m (100ft)

DID YOU KNOW?

Coal is made of prehistoric plants. During the Carboniferous (meaning coal-bearing) Period, much of Europe, North America and Asia was covered by swamps and tropical forests. As plants died, thick layers of plant material built up, forming peat. Eventually, the weight of rocks squeezed water and gases out of the peat underneath, turning it into hard, dark coal.

Christmas tree

The first Christmas trees (their real name is Norway Spruce) grew in North America 80 m.y.a.

Blooming flowers

After about 300 million years of living on land, plants began to produce flowers. The first known is the flower of the Magnolia tree which flowered at the time of the dinosaurs, just as it flowers today.

The time clock

If the first living things appeared in the seas at midday, then the first life on land appeared just five minutes before midnight. Plants lived on land before animals, because animals depend on plants for their food.

Amber traps

Fossils of insects are very rare because their bodies are so delicate. Pine trees leak a sticky liquid, called resin, which often traps insects. Prehistoric resin turns into a transparent, yellow stone, called amber, in which prehistoric insects have been found. It is mainly found on the southern coast of the Baltic Sea.

A giant sea scorpion, called Pterygotus, lived 400 m.y.a. It was about as long as a car and had huge pincers to catch its food. It is the largest known arthropod (animal with a hard, jointed, outer skeleton).

Boomerang head

Diplocaulus was an amphibian with a strange shaped head which it may have used to help it swim. Other animals would have found it difficult to swallow.

The first amphibian

Amphibians live both on land and in the water. They need to swim to keep their skins moist, and, because their eggs do not have a waterproof shell, they lay their eggs in water. The first amphibian lived 350 m.y.a. It was called Ichthyostega.

The largest insect ever

The first animals to fly were insects. They appeared 300 m.y.a. and, until flying reptiles appeared 195 m.y.a., they had the air to themselves. Some were huge, like Meganeura, a giant dragonfly. As big as a kite, it had a wing-span of 76cm (30in).

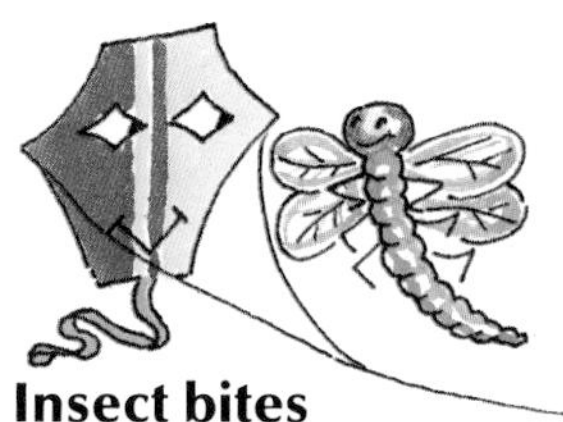

Insect bites

Some of the earliest known plants lived 380 m.y.a. and were found in Rhynie, Scotland. They have holes made by insects feeding on them. The earliest known insect, Rhyniella, was found there. It was a very small springtail.

Changing world

Earth's floating layers

The Earth's surface is made of layers, called plates, which float on liquid rock underneath. The plates move, sliding over or past each other. Where they bump, there are volcanoes and earthquakes.

A fantastic waterfall

In 1970, scientists discovered that 6 m.y.a. the Mediterranean Sea was a huge, dry valley. Then the Earth's crust moved and the Atlantic Ocean burst over the Straits of Gibraltar in the most spectacular waterfall ever. It took over a hundred years to fill the Mediterranean.

Moving continents

Over millions of years, the continents have split and moved apart, or bumped into each other and joined up.

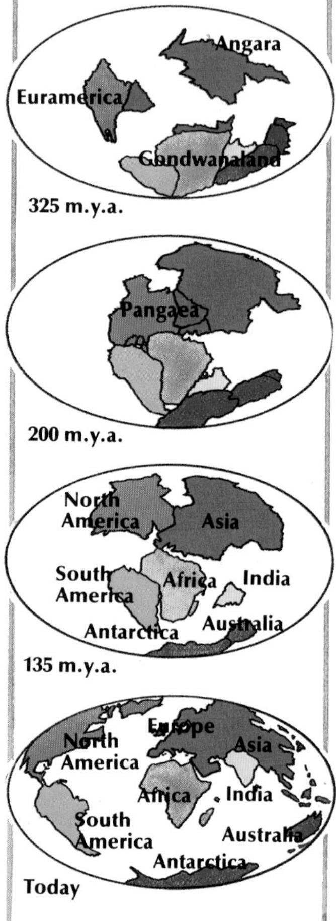

Opposite climates

One of the hottest areas in the world today is the Sahara Desert, but 450 m.y.a. it was covered by ice. The coldest place in the world today is Antarctica, but millions of years ago it had a hot, tropical climate.

Amazing But True

About 200 m.y.a., India was joined to Antarctica. It has moved nearly 7,000km (4,350 miles) to its present position.

The coal forests

Coal was formed in North America, Europe, Asia and Antarctica in the Carboniferous Period (345-280 m.y.a.). At that time these continents were near the Equator and had hot climates.

Mountain building

Europe
The Alps were formed by Africa moving north, and pushing the Mediterranean sea floor against Europe.

North America
Millions of years ago, Africa and North America joined, pushing the sea floor up to form the Appalachians. The Atlantic Ocean began separating the two continents again 180 m.y.a.

South America
The Pacific floor has sunk under the edge of South America, pushing the land up to form the Andes.

Asia
When the three ancient continents, (Angara, Euramerica, Gondwanaland), collided, they made one large continent (Pangaea). The Ural mountains formed where they met.

Getting to the top
Fossil sea-shells have been found high on the Himalayas, 500km (310 miles) away from the nearest sea. As India moved north and joined Asia, it pushed up the sea floor in between, forming the Himalayas.

A jigsaw puzzle
Animal and plant fossils, found in separate parts of the world, were clues to scientists that the continents once fitted together like a jigsaw.

The oldest rocks
The oldest things on Earth are rocks. They are 4,600 million-year-old meteorites from space which landed in Antarctica. Some of the oldest rocks formed on Earth are in Greenland. They are 3,820 million years old.

London 50 m.y.a.
About 50 m.y.a., London had a hot and humid climate. It was covered in jungle and swamps where crocodiles and turtles lived.

New York 200 m.y.a.
About 200 m.y.a., New York was part of a large lake where the earliest known gliding reptile, called Icarosaurus, lived.

Early reptiles

The first reptiles

The earliest known reptiles lived 300 m.y.a. Their fossils were found in Nova Scotia, Canada. Reptiles ruled the land for more than 200 million years.

DID YOU KNOW?

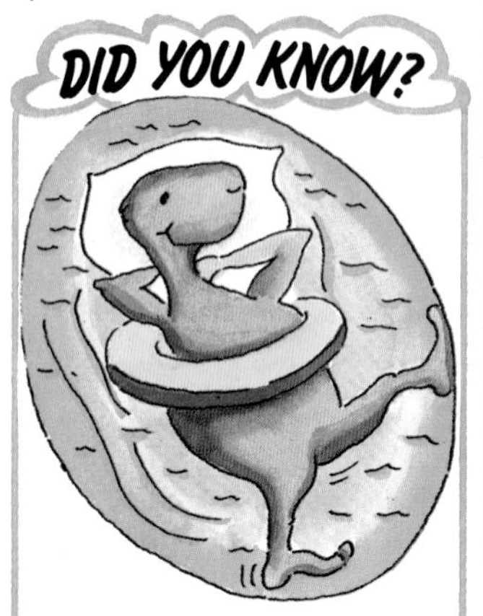

Reptiles were the first vertebrates that were able to live entirely on land. They did not have to lay their eggs in water like amphibians, because their eggs had hard, leathery shells. These stopped the liquid around the young animal inside from drying out.

The oldest eggs

The oldest known fossil eggs in the world were laid by reptiles in the Permian Period (280-230 m.y.a.). They were the size of chickens' eggs.

Sails on their backs

Dimetrodon

Fossils of two reptiles, Edaphosaurus and Dimetrodon were found in Texas. They lived 270 m.y.a. at a time when the climate was hot and dry. They had sails on their backs, made of spines covered by skin.

Keeping cool

Reptiles are cold-blooded. This means their blood temperature depends on the sun and the air around them. Reptiles used the sails on their backs like radiators, turning them towards or away from the sun when they wanted to warm up or cool down.

Edaphosaurus

Most common reptiles

Rhynchosaurs were the most common reptiles 220-195 m.y.a. They were herbivorous (they ate plants) and about the size of sheep. They are ancestors of the Tuatara lizard found today in New Zealand.

The dinosaur's ancestor

Thecodonts were early ancestors of dinosaurs. One, Erythrosuchus, was the largest animal known to have lived on land until the dinosaurs 190 m.y.a. It was about 5m long (16ft).

Cambrian Ordovician Silurian Devonian Carboniferous

The return to sea

About 210 m.y.a., three groups of reptiles left the land and returned to live in the sea. They developed powerful swimming paddles and fins, instead of legs and feet.

Ichthyosaurs were fish-like lizards, the size of dolphins. They did not lay eggs like other reptiles. Instead they gave birth to live young.

Plesiosaurs had very long necks. One of the largest, Elasmosaurus, had a neck 6m long (19ft), which was as long as its body

Sea-turtles grew to an enormous size. The largest known, called Archelon, lived 85 m.y.a. It was as large as three ping-pong tables.

The largest crocodile

The largest crocodile the world has ever known lived about 75 m.y.a. in Texas, USA. It was 16m long (52ft) and weighed as much as 170 people.

Tanystropheus had the longest neck in proportion to its body of any known animal. The neck was 4m long (13ft), twice as long as its body, and was probably used like a fishing rod to catch fish. This reptile lived about 22 m.y.a. in Europe.

Largest sea-reptile

Stretosaurus macromerus was the largest marine reptile ever to have lived. A jaw-bone found in Britain was over 3m long (10 ft). Its total length must have been as long as eight frogmen.

Permian

Dinosaur giants

Successful survivors

Dinosaurs were a group of reptiles that lived on Earth from about 200 to 65 m.y.a., a total of 140 million years. That is 70 times longer than the 2 million years that human beings are believed to have lived.

DID YOU KNOW?

Dinosaurs were first called 'dinosaurs' in 1841 by Dr Richard Owen. He used the word, which means 'terrible lizard' in Greek, for the first three known dinosaurs: Hylaeosaurus, Megalosaurus, Iguanodon.

A human giant?

Until about 150 years ago, no one knew that dinosaurs had existed. So when, in 1677, part of Megalosaurus' leg bone was discovered in England, people thought that it had belonged to a giant man.

Giants among giants

The largest land animals ever to have lived were Sauropods. They were a group of herbivorous (plant-eating) dinosaurs, and had quite small feet for such large bodies.

Sauropods	Height	Weight	Length
Diplodocus	unknown	11 tonnes	26m (85ft)
Apatosaurus	unknown	30 tonnes	21m (68ft)
Barosaurus	unknown	unknown	28m (91ft)
Cetiosaurus	unknown	9 tonnes	14m (45ft)
Brachiosaurus	13m (42ft)	100 tonnes	28m (91ft)

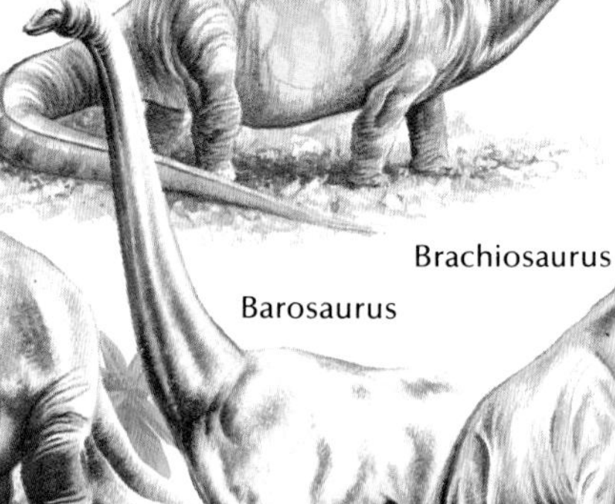

A dinosaur dinner

Dinosaur models were built in 1854 for the Crystal Palace gardens in London. The sculptor made Iguanodon look rather like a rhinoceros, and before finishing it held a dinner party in it for 20 people.

The largest skeleton

Brachiosaurus' skeleton in the Natural Science Museum, East Berlin, is the largest dinosaur skeleton in the world. It was discovered in Tanzania, and must have weighed as much as 15 large African elephants when it was alive.

A dinosaur recipe

This is what it took to build a lifesize model of Iguanodon:

600 bricks

650 tiles

38 casks of cement

90 casks of broken stone

30.5m (100ft) of iron hooping

6m (19ft) of iron bar.

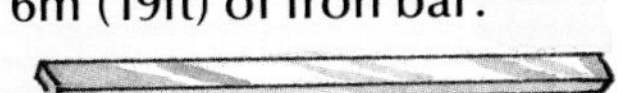

A wall of dinosaurs

Visitors to the Dinosaur National Monument in Utah, USA, can see a 58m long wall (190ft) with more than a thousand dinosaur bones embedded in it. Since 1909, train loads of fossils have been collected by scientists. This wall was once, 140 m.y.a., part of a sandy river bed in which dinosaurs became stuck and died.

Amazing But True

The largest dinosaur egg ever found was discovered in France. It was as large as a rugby ball, and was laid by a Sauropod, the huge Hypselosaurus.

The smallest dinosaur

Not all dinosaurs were huge. One of the smallest known adult dinosaurs was only 60cm long (2ft). It was found in Scotland and named 'Saltopus' (leaping foot) because it had long hind legs to help it run fast.

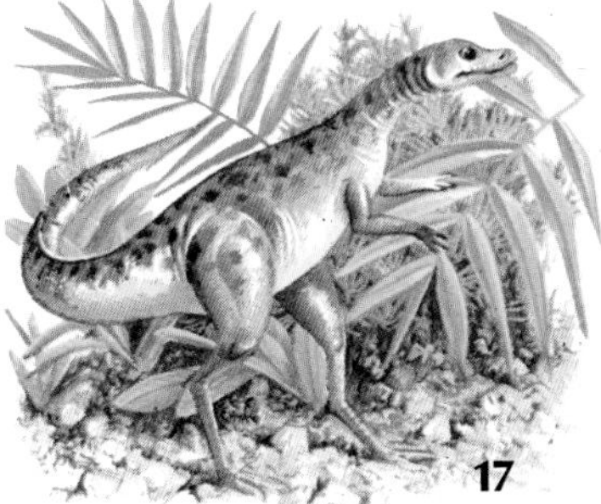

More dinosaurs

A suit of armour

Herbivorous dinosaurs needed protection from carnivorous (meat-eating) dinosaurs. Ankylosaurus had heavy, bony plates over its head, back, and tail which protected it from attack, like a suit of armour.

Amazing But True

Horned dinosaurs had frills of bone to protect their necks. Torosaurus had the largest frill of all. Its head, which measured 2.5m (8ft), was the size of a car, and the largest known of any land animal.

Triceratops

One of the last dinosaurs was Triceratops. It was 9m long (30ft) and weighed 6 tonnes. With its long horns measuring nearly 1m (3ft), few animals could have survived being charged by Triceratops.

A dinosaur's trumpet

Hadrosaurs lived 85-65 m.y.a. and were among the most common dinosaurs found in North America. One, Parasaurulophus, had a crest on its head that was almost 2m long (6ft) which it could blow like a trumpet.

'Bone Cabin'

About 100 years ago, a shepherd in Wyoming, USA, found an area of land that was covered by so many bones that he used about 500 of them to build a cabin. Later, they were found to be dinosaur, turtle, and crocodile bones.

Giving dinosaurs a name

Dinosaurs are usually given Latin or Greek names. Some are named after the place where they were found; others for their features:

Shantungosaurus	found in Shantung , China
Alamosaurus	found in Alamo, Texas, USA
Pentaceratops	Greek: 'penta' (five) 'cerat' (horns) 'ops' (around the eyes)
Deinocheirus	Greek: 'terrible hand'

Giant carnivorous dinosaurs

Mysterious arms

Only the arms and three clawed fingers have been found of Deinocheirus. This must have been a gigantic carnivorous dinosaur because the arms were 2.5m long (8ft), five times longer than a human arm.

Thousands of teeth

Hadrosaurs, nicknamed 'duck-bills' because of their broad beaks, had over 2,000 teeth. New teeth grew as others wore out.

Tryannosaurus Rex

The largest carnivore (meat-eater) that has ever lived on land was Tyrannosaurus Rex. It had a massive head and teeth that were 18cm (7in) long. Its front legs were too short even to reach its mouth, and were probably only used to help it stand up. Its brain was very small for its body size.

DID YOU KNOW?

In Colorado, USA, a town changed its name from Artesia to Dinosaur because so many dinosaur fossils were found nearby. Even the streets are named after dinosaurs.

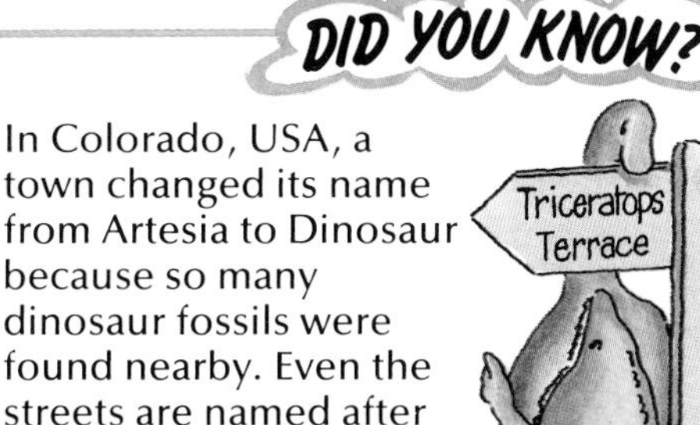

Dinosaur lifestyles

A dinosaur stampede

Footprints of over 130 stampeding dinosaurs have been found in Queensland, Australia. They had been running at a speed of 8km (5 miles) per hour, chased by a giant carnivorous dinosaur running at 15km (9 miles) per hour.

The fastest dinosaur

Not all dinosaurs were slow and clumsy. Gallimimus running on long thin hind legs may have reached speeds of 56km per hour (35 miles), nearly as fast as a racehorse.

A deadly fight

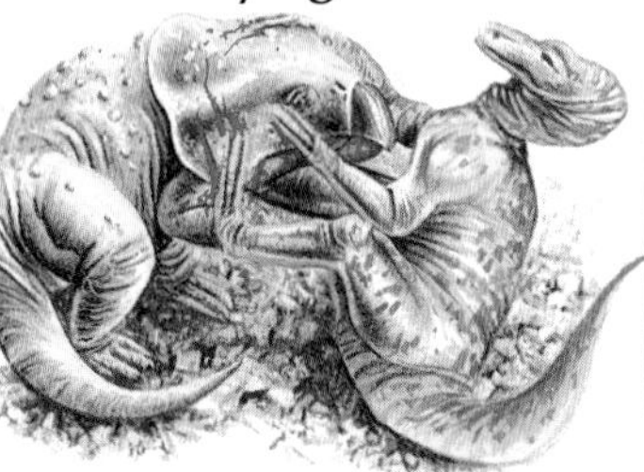

Fossils of two dinosaurs were found in the Gobi Desert, Mongolia, still locked in combat. The carnivorous Velociraptor attacked Protoceratops with its hind limbs, and died still holding on with its front limbs.

Dinosaur finds

Fossils have been found all over the world.

Stegosaurus had the smallest brain of any animal compared to its size. Its body was 6m long (19ft) and it weighed nearly 2 tonnes, but its brain was only the size of a walnut.

A dinosaur nest

Dinosaurs made nests for their eggs. Up to 18 Protoceratops eggs have been found laid in a circle in a bowl-shaped hole. Some dinosaurs may have covered their eggs with sand and left them to hatch. Maiasaura's nests were hollowed-out mounds of mud about 2m wide (6ft).

Big feet

The largest dinosaur footprints ever found were discovered in Texas, USA. They were made by a Sauropod walking in what was then soft mud. They are so large that each print can hold as much water as a bath.

Dinosaur herds

Dinosaurs may have lived in herds. Over 100 Coelophysis skeletons were found together in New Mexico in 1947 and 31 Iguanodon skeletons in a Belgian mine in 1877.

DID YOU KNOW?

Over 800 species of dinosaurs have been discovered. Scientists have divided them into two groups, depending on their hip-bone shape.

Saurischian (lizard-hipped)

Ornithischian (bird-hipped)

Bonehead

Pachycephalosaurus was the largest of a group of dinosaurs, nicknamed 'boneheads' because of their thick skulls. These were up to 25cm thick (10in), and acted like crash helmets when they fought each other.

Stomach stones

Some Sauropods have been found with large stones inside their skeletons where their stomachs would have been. They may have swallowed the stones to help grind up the leaves and twigs in their stomachs.

Animals in the sky

The largest egg ever

The eggs of the giant flightless bird, Aepyornis, are the largest of any animal that has ever lived. Each can hold 9 litres (16pts) and is equivalent to:

4 large dinosaur eggs

7 ostrich eggs

40 goose eggs

110 duck eggs

180 chicken eggs

470 pigeon eggs

12,000 hummingbird eggs

The first true bird

The earliest known true bird was Hesperornis. It was a huge sea-bird and lived about 80 m.y.a. It was about 2m long (6ft) and, unlike modern birds, had teeth. It only had one bone in its arm, so it could not have flown, but it must have been a powerful swimmer.

Reptile or bird?

The earliest known animal with feathers lived 140 m.y.a. and is called Archaeopteryx. It was discovered in 1861 in Germany. It had feathers and a wishbone like a bird but teeth, claws on its wings, and a long, bony tail, like a reptile.

DID YOU KNOW?

Birds may be the living descendants of dinosaurs. Archaeopteryx, which had both bird and reptile features, may have been a step in the evolution of dinosaurs to birds.

Flying reptiles

The first flying animals to exist after insects were flying reptiles called Pterosaurs that lived 195-70 m.y.a. Two kinds of Pterosaurs were Rhamphorhynchus and Pterodactyls.

Largest flying animal

The largest animal ever to fly was Quetzalcoatlus northropi , a flying reptile which lived in North America 65 m.y.a. It was the size of a two-seater airplane, with a wingspan of 12m (39ft).

Giant flying reptile

Pteranodon was a huge flying reptile with a wingspan of 7m (23ft). The bony horn on its head was 1m long (3ft) and balanced the weight of its enormous beak.

Dromornis stirtoni is the largest bird ever to have lived. It was 3m tall (10ft) and weighed 500kg (1100lb), which is nearly four times heavier than an ostrich, the largest living bird. It did not have wings. It lived in Australia 10-11 m.y.a.

The largest flying bird

The largest bird ever to fly was Argentavis magnificens. It had a wingspan of 7m (23ft) and weighed about 120kg (265lb). It probably did not fly by flapping its wings, but may have lifted itself off the ground by spreading its wings in the direction of the wind and then remained in the air, like a glider, by using the air currents.

Bird firsts

	First lived		First lived
Flamingoes	70 m.y.a.	Ostriches	45 m.y.a.
Owls	70 m.y.a.	Ducks	30 m.y.a.
Hawks	45 m.y.a.	Pelicans	16 m.y.a.
Penguins	45 m.y.a.	Geese	16 m.y.a.

The arrival of mammals

Making mammals

During the Triassic Period, about 200 m.y.a., mammal-like reptiles were developing into mammals. Thrinaxodon was a reptile that had teeth and ribs like a mammal, and must have moved like one.

DID YOU KNOW?

Animals which have fur or hair, and feed their babies with their own milk are called mammals. Mammals are warm-blooded animals which means that they are able to keep their body temperature about the same, whatever the outside temperature.

The first mammals

The two earliest known mammals lived 190 m.y.a. Morganucodon was found in Wales and Megazostrodon in Lesotho. They may have laid eggs like their reptile ancestors, and not given birth to live young like most modern mammals.

The largest whale

The largest prehistoric sea mammal was a giant whale, Basilosaurus, that lived 40 m.y.a. It was 20m long (65ft) but smaller than the Blue Whale, the largest living whale, which can be up to 27m long (88ft).

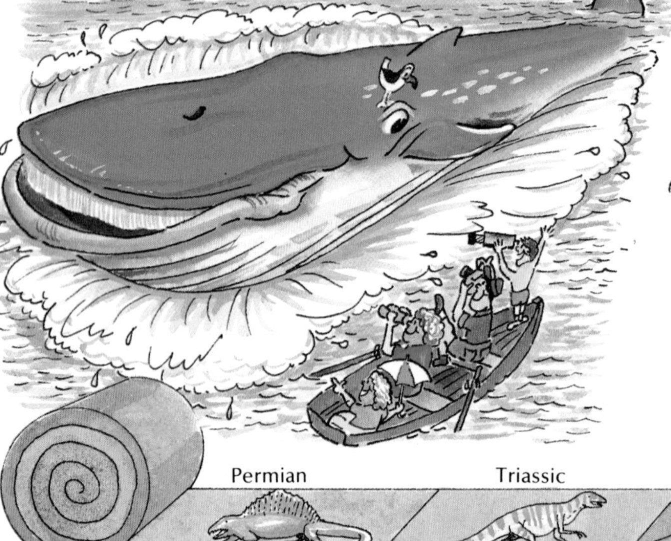

Big pockets

Two giant prehistoric marsupials lived in Australia. Marsupials give birth to tiny babies that live in their mother's stomach pouch until they are grown. Diprotodon was a wombat as big as a rhinoceros. Procoptodon was a huge kangaroo: it was over 3m tall (10ft).

Permian Triassic Jurassic Cretaceous

Prehistoric head gear

Megaceros lived in Europe 3,000 years ago. The male's antlers had the widest span of any known animal: they were 3m wide (10ft) and weighed 50kg (110lb).

Arsinoitherium, lived in North Africa 35 m.y.a.

Uintatherium lived in North America 45 m.y.a.

Brontotherium, lived in North America 35 m.y.a.

Elasmotherium lived in the USSR 200,000 years ago. Its horn could be up to 2m long (6ft).

Synthetoceras lived in North America 15 m.y.a.

Tall and small camels

Alticamelus was a camel with a giraffe's neck. It was 3.5m tall (11ft) and lived in North America 10 m.y.a. Stenomylus was a tiny camel, only as big as a gazelle.

Amazing But True

The largest land mammal that has ever lived was Paraceratherium, found in Baluchistan in 1912. It was 8m tall (26ft) and 11m long (36ft). It had a body like a rhinoceros, a head like a horse, legs like an elephant and a tail like a donkey.

Tertiary

Quarternary

More mammals

Los Angeles' tar pools

Thousands of mammal fossils, the most ever found in one place, were found at Ranch La Brea in Los Angeles, USA. Animals who came to drink at a pool there 15,000 years ago became stuck in tar that seeped from the ground. Most were carnivores; they came to attack animals trapped in the tar, and were also trapped. Over 1,600 dire wolves and 1,000 sabre-tooth cats were found, as well as ground sloths, camels, mammoths, and horses.

Tar still seeps through the ground and traps animals there; these may be fossils in thousands of years.

Placental mammals (like human beings, rabbits, whales) keep their young inside their bodies until they are well developed. For the last 65 m.y.a., 95% of all mammals have been placental.

Giant mammals

Many mammals living today had giant ancestors. There were giant rhinoceroses, wart hogs, and beavers.

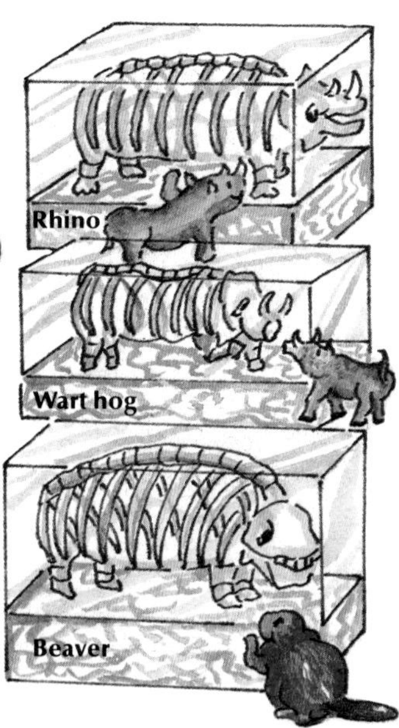

The longest tusks

The longest tusks ever discovered belonged to a prehistoric elephant found in Germany. They were 5m long (16ft), which is nearly twice as long as the tusks of living elephants.

Stabbing teeth

One of the fiercest carnivorous mammals was Smilodon, a huge sabre-tooth cat that lived in North America 11 m.y.a. It was as large as a lion, and its long, stabbing teeth were as long as this page.

Big mouth

Megistotherium is the largest known carnivorous mammal ever. It lived in North Africa 20 m.y.a. It weighed about 900kg (1,984lb), and had a huge head, about twice the size of any bear's head and could attack the largest elephants with its long, sharp teeth.

Horses

The first horses lived in the North American forests. They were only the size of cats, and had toes on their feet. The first horse to have hoofs was Pliohippus.

Pliohippus 5 m.y.a.

Hyracotherium 55 m.y.a.

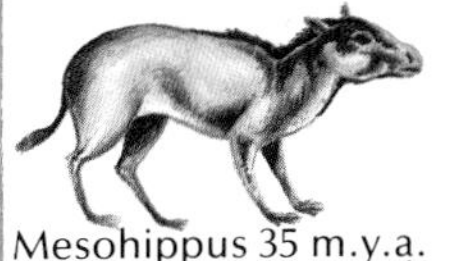

Mesohippus 35 m.y.a.

Merychippus 20 m.y.a.

Equus 2 m.y.a.

Amazing But True

The first elephants were only the size of sheep. Moeritherium weighed about 20kg (44lb) and was about 300 times smaller than an African elephant, the largest land animal alive today.

Shovels and forks

Platybelodon used its lower jaw like a shovel to pick up food and water. It lived 20 m.y.a. in Europe. Deinotherium was an elephant which had tusk-like lower teeth which it used like a fork to dig for roots.

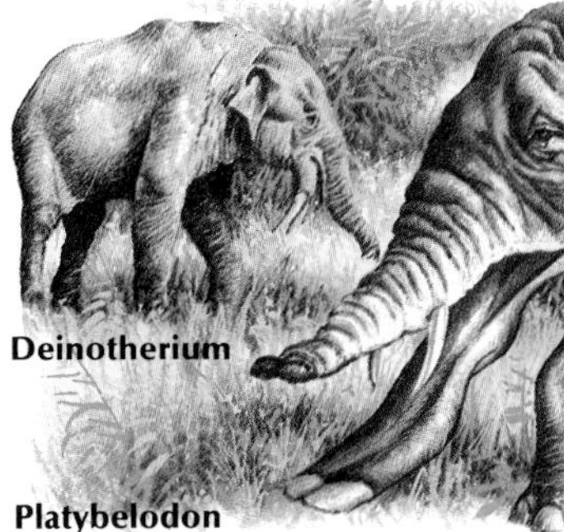

Dwarf mammals

About 1 m.y.a., dwarf species of Palaeoloxodon elephants lived on some Mediterranean islands. Those that lived on the mainland of Europe were about 5m tall (16ft), but those living on islands, such as Malta, were only 1m tall (3ft).

Mammoth mammals

Mammoth facts

The largest mammoth was as large as a tank with huge, curved tusks 4m long (13ft). They lived from 5 m.y.a. until 10,000 years ago. Woolly mammoths had long hair and a thick undercoat for warmth. Their teeth were the size of bricks.

Amazing But True

The frozen ground of Siberia, USSR, is like a giant deep-freeze. Many animals have been perfectly preserved in it. In the last 300 years, 4,700 frozen mammoths have been found there and 500,000 tonnes of mammoth tusks may still lie buried along the coast.

Mini mammoth

In 1977, a perfectly preserved baby mammoth was discovered in the USSR, in the frozen ground of Siberia. Just 1m tall (3ft), it was about 7 months old when it died 40,000 years ago.

Woolly coats

Mammals had to adapt to survive the cold of the Ice Age. Giant forms of mammoths, oxen, horses, elephants, and bison developed because their larger bodies were better at conserving heat. Rhinoceroses and mammoths also grew woolly coats.

Woolly rhinoceros

Woolly mammoth

The British scene

The British climate was much warmer during the last interglacial period than at present. Listed here are mammals found in a cave at Joint Mitnor, Devon. They had fallen through a hole in the ground 12,000 years ago:

Hippopotamus
Bison
Giant deer
Red deer
Bear
Lion
Hyena
Wolf
Elephant
Rhinoceros

South American specialities

For 60 million years, until 2 m.y.a., South America was separated from North America. Many mammals, unknown in the rest of the world, developed there.

Glyptodon was 2.5m long (8ft). Its shell was solid bone and it probably used its heavy tail for defence.

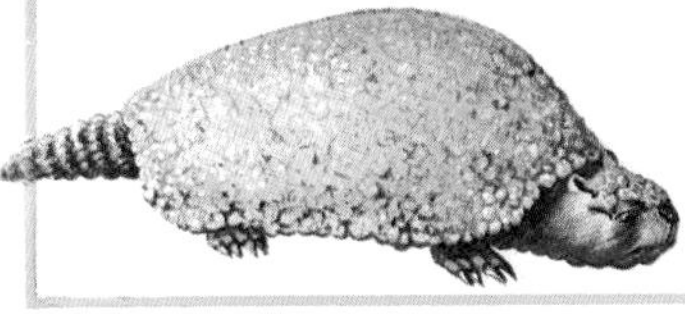

Megatherium was a giant sloth that lived 2 m.y.a. With the help of a strong tail for balance, it was able to stand 6m (19ft) tall to reach its food of tree leaves.

The oldest ape of all

The oldest known ape is Aegyptopithecus. Its fossils were found in Fayum, on the edge of the Egyptian desert. When it lived there 27 m.y.a., the land was covered in thick tropical forest.

Mammoth meal

A complete frozen mammoth found in 1900 in Siberia, still had 14kg (30lbs) of undigested food in its stomach. Its meat was so well preserved 30,000 years after being frozen that people were able to eat some of it.

Human beings, apes, and monkeys all belong to a group of mammals called primates. Plesiadapis lived 60 m.y.a. and was among the first primates.

A cave of bear bones

Huge cave bears lived in Europe between 700,000 and 12,000 years ago. They stayed in caves during the Ice Age winters. In one cave in Austria where bears had sheltered over thousands of years, the bones of over 30,000 were discovered. Prehistoric people hunted them by trapping them in caves.

Ice ages

Ancient Ice Ages

There have been many Ice Ages. The first known occurred 2,300 m.y.a. in North America. Several more Ice Ages between 1,000 and 600 m.y.a. have left traces all over the world. Between 345-270 m.y.a., the southern half of the world cooled.

Ice flowing downhill in the Himalayas, Andes, and Alps scraped valleys sometimes 31km deep (21 miles) removing millions of tonnes of rock. Spreading ice during a glacial period sometimes trapped rocks, moving them huge distances. Such rocks (called erratics) in southern England came from Norway.

DID YOU KNOW?

We are living today in the Quaternary Ice Age which began 3 m.y.a. During this time, there have been 17 cold (glacial) and 17 warm (interglacial) periods. Only 10% of the last 2 million years have been interglacial. Ours began 10,000 years ago.

Ice sheets

During the last glacial period 19,000 years ago, a huge sheet of ice covered a third of the Earth's surface, and icebergs floated in half of the seas. Today, only Greenland and Antarctica are covered by ice which has been there since 3 m.y.a. The Arctic Ocean has been frozen for 700,000 years.

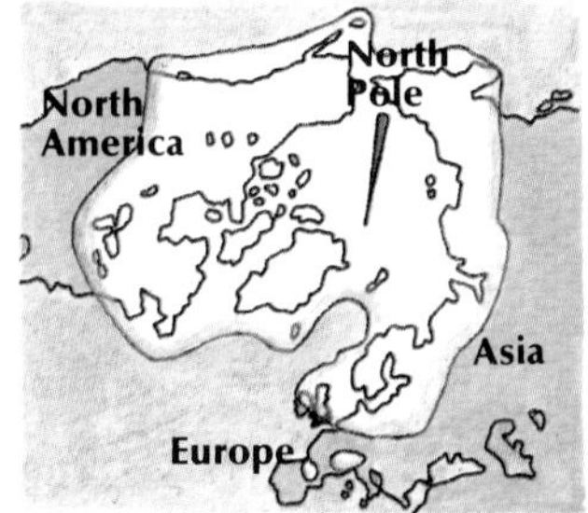

Bridges of land

As sea water turned to ice in the last glacial period, the world's sea level lowered at a rate of 12m (39ft) every 1,000 years. This created land bridges between land that had been separated by sea. Animals could then migrate to other continents.

The big freezes

Ice Ages happen when the Earth moves away from the Sun. Every 90,000 years the Earth

travels on a longer orbit around the Sun. Every 40,000 years the Earth's axis tilts away from the Sun and every 10,000 years another change makes the southern half of the world colder than the north.

Extinction

Past and present

About 99.5% of all plant and animal species that have ever lived are now extinct. There are about 5 million species living today, but had nothing become extinct, there would be 980 million.

Mass extinctions

Many groups of animals have disappeared suddenly at different times throughout the Earth's history. Mass extinctions occurred at the end of the Permian and Cretaceous Periods.

Permian extinction

(230 m.y.a.)

75% of amphibian species

80% of reptile species

Cretaceous extinction

(65 m.y.a.)

Dinosaurs

Ichthyosaurs

Plesiosaurs

Pterosaurs

Ammonites

Dinosaur extinctions

There are about 50 theories about why, over millions of years, dinosaurs became extinct, but no one really knows the reason why. These are a few theories:

Froze to death after meteor struck Earth, producing dust cloud that blocked out Sun.

Starved to death when plague of caterpillars ate all their plant food.

Carnivorous dinosaurs ate all herbivorous dinosaurs and so had no food left.

Small mammals ate all their eggs.

Poisoned by the first flowering plants.

Egg shells became too thin and broke before dinosaurs hatched.

Grew tired of life on Earth and died of boredom.

Our ancestors

Early Ape

From 14 to 8 m.y.a.

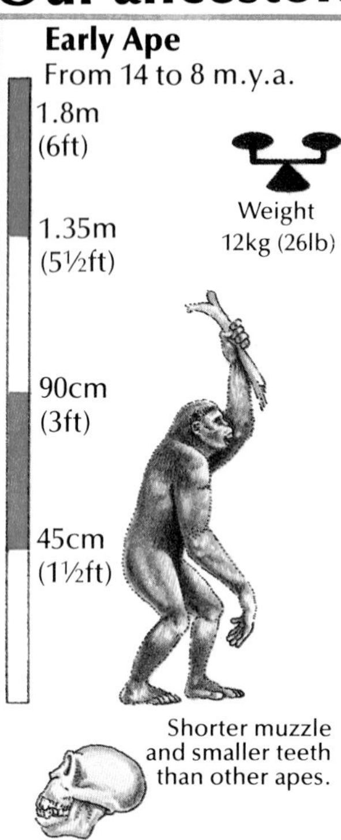

Shorter muzzle and smaller teeth than other apes.

Ramapithecus

This Early Ape is the first homonid (man-type) and our oldest direct ancestor. The first fossil was discovered in India and named after Rama, an Indian god.

Time compared

If the 2 million years since the first human beings existed are compared to 1 year, the first civilisation began after 5p.m. on the 30th December.

Man-ape

From 5 to 1½ m.y.a.

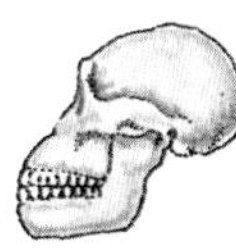

Thick, bony ridge above eyes. Small skull.

Australopithecus

The oldest homonid footprints in the world were made 3¾ m.y.a. in Tanzania by these man-like apes. They were made by 2 adults and a child and look exactly like footprints made by people today.

Nutcracker Man

One type of Man-ape was nicknamed 'Nutcracker Man' because of its huge molar teeth, 3 to 4 times bigger than ours. It had special strong muscles to work its big jaws.

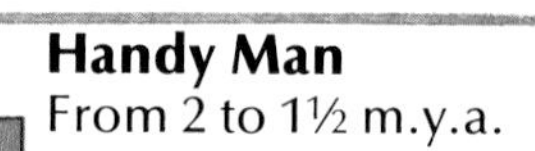

Handy Man

From 2 to 1½ m.y.a.

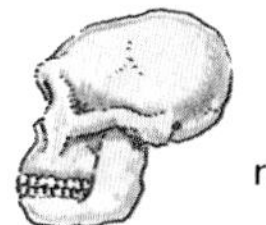

Larger brain than Man-ape, and skull rounder on top.

Homo habilis

This first true human being is named 'homo habilis', meaning 'Handy Man', because he made the first known tools. These were stones with sharp edges for cutting.

The oldest home

The earliest known shelter, made by human beings 2 m.y.a., was found in Tanzania. All that remains is a circle of stones.

Upright Man

From 1.5 to 200,000 years ago

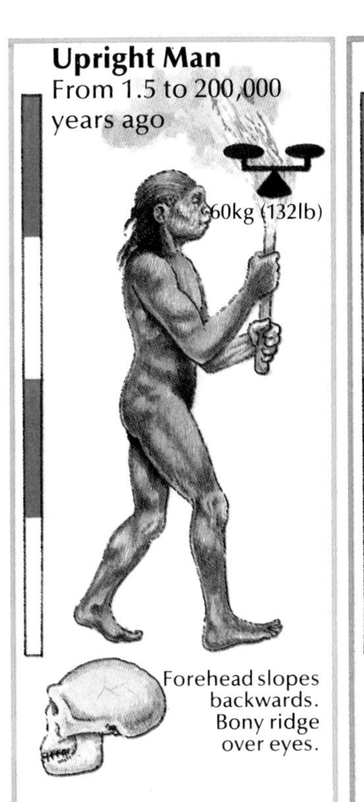

Forehead slopes backwards. Bony ridge over eyes.

Homo erectus

Upright People hunted large animals and used fire for cooking and keeping warm.

The first fire

The first fires were probably started by lightning. Peking Man (a type of Upright Man) kept fires burning in the Choukoutien caves in China about 460,000 years ago.

Neanderthal Man

From 200,000 to 40,000 years ago.

Large skull, bun shape at back. Ridge over eyes and no forehead.

Homo sapiens neanderthalensis

Neanderthal Man had a bigger brain than Modern Man's – although this does not mean he was more intelligent.

The Neanderthal skeleton discovered in 1856 in Germany was the first human fossil that was recognised to have belonged to an earlier type of man. Few people then wanted to believe our ancestors were apes.

Modern Man

From 40,000 years ago to present.

70kg (155lb)

A distinct chin and forehead. A higher and rounder skull.

Homo sapiens sapiens

Every human being alive today belongs to this species.

Longer life

In Britain, 4,500 years ago, people lived for an average of 20 to 25 years. Today the average life is 70 years.

Famous finds

1 The greatest hoax

There was great excitement in 1912, when a human fossil, Piltdown Man, was found in Britain. Then 40 years later, it turned out to be a fake. The skull's jaw was a 500 year-old orang-utang jaw.

2 The oldest Briton

Swanscombe Man is 280,000 years old, the oldest human fossil known in Britain.

4 Neanderthal Man

Neanderthal Man was named after the river in Germany by which the skeleton was found. 'Neanderthal' means 'valley of the Neander'.

5 The oldest European

The fossils of Heidelberg Man (Upright Man) are 360,000 years old, the oldest known in Europe.

8 Dragon Bone Cave

The Chinese used to grind bones they found in the Choukoutien caves into medicine powder, thinking they were dragon bones. In 1927, the bones were found to be those of Peking Man (Upright Man) and of the animals he had hunted.

3 The skeleton song

The most complete Man-ape skeleton was found at Olduvai, Tanzania. It was called 'Lucy' because the fossil-hunters played the record 'Lucy in the Sky with Diamonds' when celebrating their find.

6 Rift Valley fossils

The climate and soil in the Rift Valley, Africa, where many fossils are found, is ideal for fossilization.

7 First modern person

The first modern skull, Cromagnon Man, was found in France and is about 25,000 years old.

9 First ocean travellers

About 30,000 years ago, the first people reached Australia. At that time, they would have had to cross at least 60km (37 miles) of open sea.

10 Disappearing bones

During World War 2, fossils of Peking Man (who lived 500,000 years ago) were to be sent to the USA for safe-keeping. They were carefully packed, put on a train, and never seen again. They mystery of their disappearance has never been solved.

14 The first Americans

The first people probably reached North America about 30,000 years ago by crossing the Bering Strait from Asia. The Bering Strait was then dry land. These people were the ancestors of the American Indians.

16 Moving south

Anthropologists (people who study human ancestors, societies, and customs) believe that the first human beings in America spread quickly from north to south in search of animals to hunt.

Arctic Ocean

Greenland

North America

11

16

Atlantic Ocean

South America

15

17 African beginnings

So far, Africa is the only continent where our earliest human ancestors (Man-ape and Handy Man) have been discovered.

Land-bridges

Land-bridges are shown on the map. They are areas that were joined by dry land when the sea-level was lower during the last Ice Age.

11 Oldest Americans

The oldest human fossils found in the USA are 12,000 years old.

12 Java Man

Discovered in 1891, this was the first Upright Man ever found.

13 The first Australians

Only a few fossils of the first Australians have been found. Many sites where they lived were covered by the sea when the sea level rose at the end of the last Ice Age.

15 The end of the road

People reached the tip of South America by about 12,000 years ago.

Where our ancestors have been found

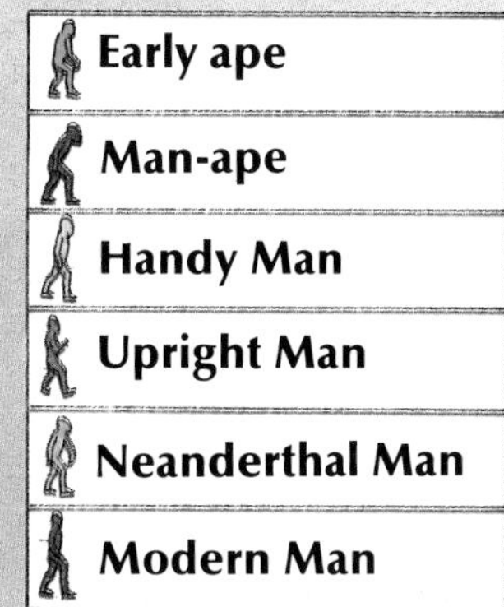

Finding food

Human beings have lived on Earth for at least 2 million years. The first people to grow crops lived 10,000 years ago. Before that they found food by hunting wild animals and gathering wild fruits. These people are called hunter-gatherers.

The first domesticated plants

	years ago	place
Wheat	10,000	Iraq
Barley	10,000	Turkey
Avocados	9,000	Mexico
Peas	8,500	Turkey
Beans	8,000	Peru
Rice	8,000	Thailand
Corn	7,500	Mexico
Millet	6,500	China
Soya beans	5,000	China
Potatoes	4,000	Argentina

Less for more

One hunter-gatherer would have needed about 25 sq km of land (10 sq miles) to provide enough food. The same amount of land would have produced enough food for about 26 early farmers.

Who's for dinner?

Some of our ancestors may have been cannibals. The skulls of Upright Men found in China had all been broken as if to take out the brains, and the bones smashed for the marrow inside. Eating brains and marrow may have been part of a ritual to honour a dead person, rather than a way of getting food.

Man's oldest friend

Dogs have been kept by people for at least 10,000 years. They were probably used for hunting and to drive herds of animals.

Upright Man's Menu

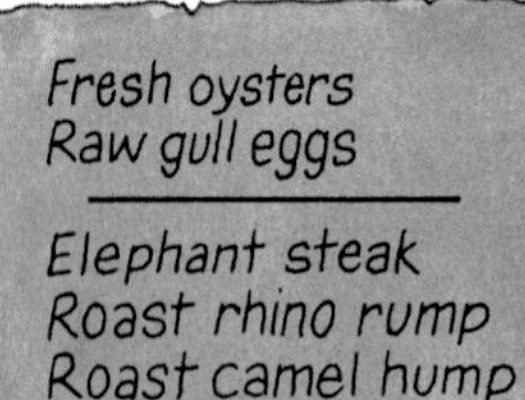

Neanderthal Man's Menu

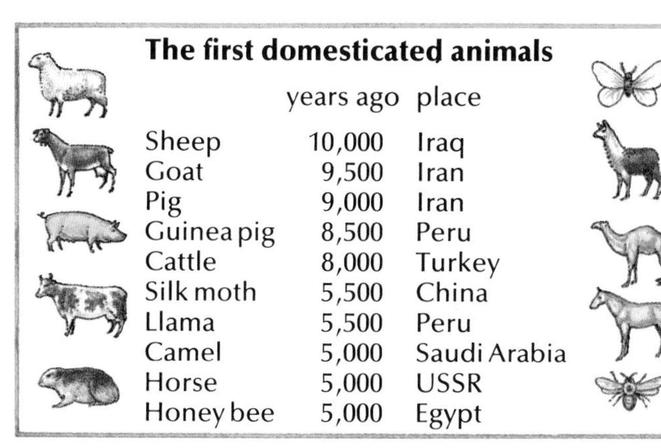

The first domesticated animals

	years ago	place
Sheep	10,000	Iraq
Goat	9,500	Iran
Pig	9,000	Iran
Guinea pig	8,500	Peru
Cattle	8,000	Turkey
Silk moth	5,500	China
Llama	5,500	Peru
Camel	5,000	Saudi Arabia
Horse	5,000	USSR
Honey bee	5,000	Egypt

On the move for food

Hunter-gatherers had to follow the herds of wild animals they hunted, so they could not live in one place. The animals provided about a third of their food. For the rest, they collected fruits, seeds, nuts, and roots.

Beer was being brewed 8,000 years ago in the Near East and bread was being baked at least 10,000 years ago.

Now and then

Plants and animals grown and bred by people are called domesticated. Over the years, they change from their wild ancestors.

Wild and farmed species

Wild and farmed pigs

Wild and farmed wheat

Wild and farmed sheep

The first farms

Farming began in the Near East about 10,000 years ago, in South America about 9,000 years ago, and in East Asia about 7,000 years ago.

Useful animals

People domesticated animals for their meat, for their milk, for their hide and wool, and also to carry loads.

Early Modern Man's Menu

Early Farmer's Menu

Making things

Old Stone Age or Palaeolithic Age

(palaeolithic = 'old stone' in Greek

Prehistory is divided into Ages, according to the tools made by early people that have been found. These tools developed at different times in different places.

Lower Palaeolithic

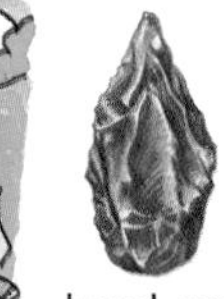

hand-axe

From 600,000 to 220,000 years ago, represented by Upright Man.

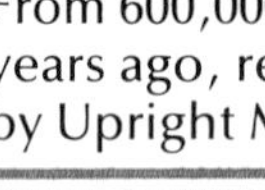

Middle Palaeolithic

flake tool

From 22,000 to 35,000 years ago, represented by Neanderthal Man.

Upper Palaeolithic

harpoon

From 35,000 to 12,000 years ago, represented by Modern Man.

Middle Stone Age or Mesolithic

(mesolithic = 'middle stone' in Greek)

The Middle Stone Age began about 12,000 years ago in the Near East, and about 10,000 years ago in Britain. People made a greater variety of tools.

blade

dug-out boat

spear thrower

points

bone comb

fish trap

borer

arrow head

bone needle

New Stone Age or Neolithic Age

(neolithic = 'new stone' in Greek)

People learnt to produce their own food by domesticating plants and animals; they settled in villages but they still used only stone, wooden, or bone tools. The plough was invented 6,000 years ago in the Near East. The first ploughs were forked branches with sharp points pulled by men. These people made clay pots and ladles, and carved elaborate daggers.

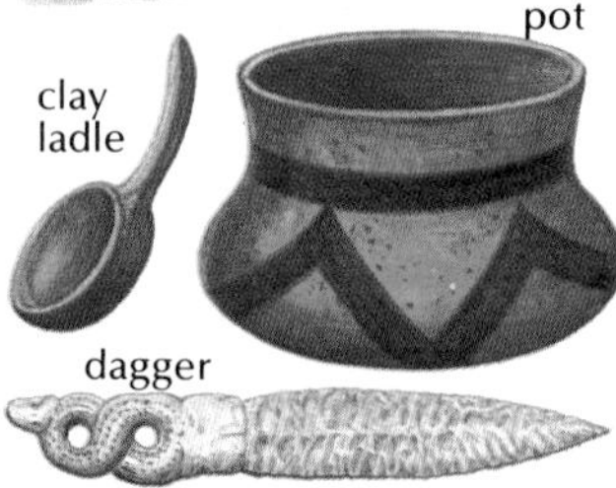

pot

clay ladle

dagger

A round revolution

The wheel was invented about 5,500 years ago in the Near East. The first wheels were made from 3 pieces of wood.

Start of New Stone Age

Place	Years ago
Near East	10,000
North Africa	10,000
Southern Europe	8,000
Central Europe	6,500
Britain	6,000

Hunting

Many of the tools made by early people were used for cutting meat or hunting animals.

The first potters

Clay pots which are 7,000 years old have been discovered in Iraq.

The oldest skis

Skis made during the Upper Palaeolithic were found in the USSR. They were made from bone, and decorated with an elk-head design.

The Metal Ages

The Copper Age began:

Near East	9,000 years ago
Europe	5,000 years ago

The Bronze Age began:

Near East	6,000 years ago
Europe	4,000 years ago

The Iron Age began:

Europe	2,900 years ago
Near East	2,600 years ago

The first metal tools

For 98% of the time human beings have been on Earth, they have lived in the Stone Ages, using stone, wood, and bone tools. They learnt to make tools from copper about 9,900 years ago in the Near East.

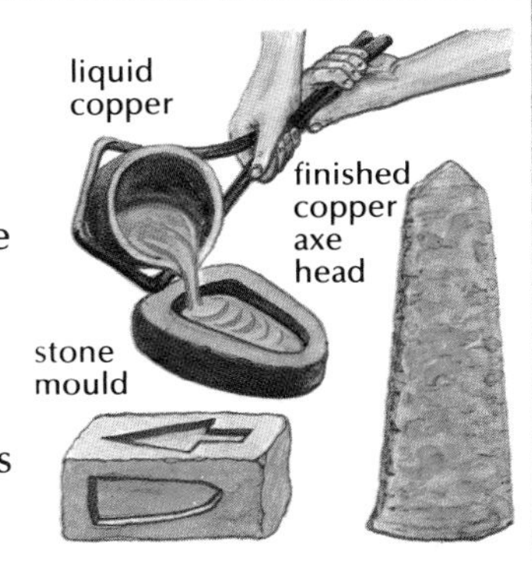

DID YOU KNOW?

There are still people who live by hunting and gathering food, and who still use simple Stone Age tools.

Early music

Flutes and whistles were used 20,000 years ago, either to make music or as signals during hunts. Flutes were made of bird and bear bones, and whistles from the toe bones of deer.

The first sails

Sailing boats were first used in the Near East, 5,000 years ago.

The oldest cloth

Pieces of the oldest cloth in the world were found in Israel in 1983. They are 9,000 years old and woven in 11 patterns.

The oldest clothes

A 37,000 year old body was found in frozen soil in Siberia, wearing a shirt and trousers. They were made from skins and stitched with thongs.

Building things

Britain's famous circle

Stonehenge was begun nearly 4,800 years ago. It was built over a period of about 1,700 years. Blocks of stone, each weighing over 50 tonnes, were brought from 40km away (25 miles). It would have taken at least 1,000 men to drag each stone. The 'blue stones', which make the cross pieces, came from Wales, 220km away (137 miles).

A field of menhirs

Prehistoric people erected 4,000 menhirs (large standing stones) about 4,500 years ago, near Carnac, in France. Today 2,000 menhirs still stand in parallel lines which stretch for 6km (4 miles). No one knows why these stones were put here.

The first farmers

The first villages to be lived in permanently were in the Near East. This is because people there learnt to grow the wheat and barley that grew wild in the region. Once people could grow food in their own area, they could settle in one place.

All the buildings and monuments on this page were built by people using very simple tools, without using wheels.

The oldest buildings

Remains of a 450,000 year old hut, built by Upright Man, were found at Terra Amata, near Nice in France. The oldest buildings still standing are the megalithic temples of Malta, which are 5,250 years old. (Megalith means 'large stone' in Greek).

The largest barrow

Huge mounds, called barrows, were built over graves. Europe's largest barrow is Silbury Hill in Britain. It covers an area of 22,000m^2 (236,806ft^2) and is 40m high (132ft). About 670,000 tonnes of chalky earth were moved to make it. It would have taken the equivalent of 3,700 men two years to build, working an eight-hour day, for 300 days of the year.

Mammoth bone huts

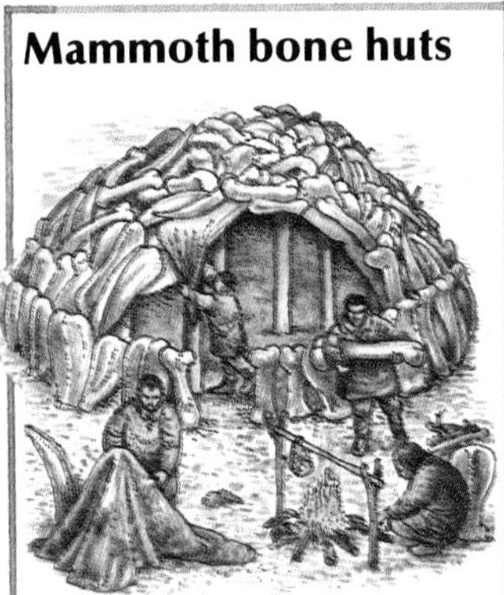

About 15,000 years ago, mammoth-hunters in the Ukraine, USSR, built their houses out of mammoth bones. One of the most famous is near the town of Mezhirich. It probably took 10 people 6 days to build it.

The pyramid builders

The Great Pyramid was built in Egypt as a tomb for King Khufu. It is 146m high (480ft) and covers an area of 52,600m^2 (566,181ft^2). Stone blocks, weighing up to 15 tonnes, were dragged to the site, and cut into 2 million 2½ tonne cubes. These were pulled up mud ramps (which were later removed). Although it was built 4,500 years ago, this is not truly a prehistoric building because it was built after the Egyptians began to write and to record their history.

Bricks and walls

Jericho, in Jordan, is the first town known to have had an outer wall for defence. It was 3m thick (10 ft) and 4m high (13ft). The world's oldest brick was found there and is 8,000 years old. It was made of mud, shaped by hand and dried in the sun.

The biggest menhir

Some of the largest menhirs are found at Locmariaquer in France. They weigh nearly 350 tonnes which is as heavy as 35 African elephants.

Neanderthal Men were the first people to bury ceremonially their dead. Fossil flower seeds were found at a grave in a cave at Shanidar, Iraq. They show that hollyhocks, cornflowers, grape hyacinths, and other flowers had been carefully placed around the body of a Neanderthal Man.

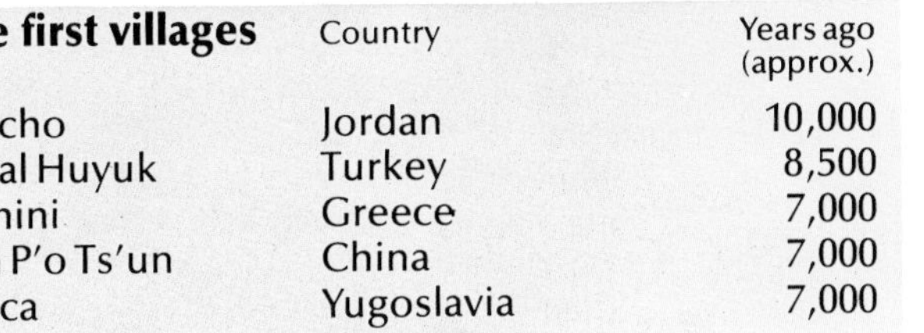

The first villages	Country	Years ago (approx.)
Jericho	Jordan	10,000
Catal Huyuk	Turkey	8,500
Dimini	Greece	7,000
Pan P'o Ts'un	China	7,000
Vinca	Yugoslavia	7,000

Artists and writers

Cave painters

The oldest paintings in the world are on cave walls in France and Spain and are 30,000 years old. Cave paintings have been found in Europe, Africa, and Australia. Most of the paintings found in Europe are in deep caves, in places difficult to reach; the pictures are nearly all of animals, such as mammoths, horses, bison, oxen, and deer. The painters may have believed that the pictures would help them catch the animals they hunted.

Prehistoric paint-box

Cave-painters made paints from minerals ground into powder. They mixed the powder with water or fat, and painted with brushes or pads of animal fur. Sometimes they blew on the powder using hollow bones. They made red, yellow, and brown from ochre, a mineral found in clay, and black from charcoal.

The first jewellery

The oldest necklaces in the world were found at Dolni Vestonice in Czechoslovakia and are 35,000 years old. Early Modern People made them from mammoth tusks, snail shells, and the teeth of arctic foxes, wolves, and bears.

The first map

The oldest map in the world was found in the USSR and is 15,000 years old. It is a map carved by mammoth-hunters on to mammoth ivory and shows their camp at Mezhirich with its huts, river, and trees.

The first sculptures

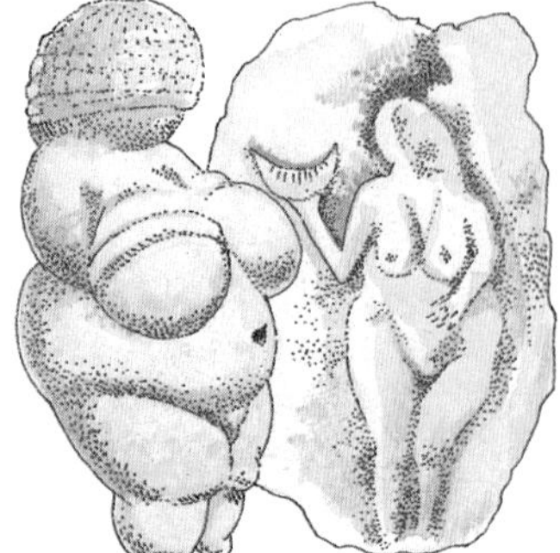

Venus of Willendorf   Venus of Laussel

The oldest sculpture was found in Austria. Called the Venus of Willendorf, it is 30,000 years old. Prehistoric sculptures were often of very fat or pregnant women – the most famous is the Venus of Laussel, found in France. People may have believed the statues brought them luck.

The oldest song

The oldest known music was played for the first time in nearly 4,000 years at a concert in the USA in 1974. The music has been deciphered but not the words. The song was written by the people of Ugarit who lived on the Syrian coast.

The oldest record

The oldest evidence of people keeping records is about 30,000 years old and was found in Cromagnon, France. There, bones were found that had been engraved with groups of lines. People may have engraved them to record the cycle of the moon, or perhaps the number of animals killed in a hunt.

The first speakers

To understand when our ancestors learnt to speak, scientists have taken plaster moulds of fossil skulls. They believe that, although all our ancestors could make noises, Modern Men, between 35,000 and 20,000 years ago, were the first capable of making the variety of sounds used in modern languages.

Our alphabet was invented by the Romans, but our numbers are taken from the Arab system who adopted it from the Hindus.

The first board game

This was found in the ancient city of Ur (Iraq) and is 5,000 years old. It is a board with 20 squares, 7 black and 7 white counters, and 6 pyramid-shaped dice.

The oldest computer

The abacus was invented over 5,000 years ago in China and is still in use in the Far East today. Each bead represents units of tens, hundreds, etc. Calculations are made by moving the beads along the wires.

The first writing

The first words were written about 5,500 years ago in Sumer (Iraq). There were no separate letters; each word was a picture of an object. People scratched them on wet clay tablets which were then dried.

Later, writers used a wedge-shaped stick to mark the clay. This writing is called cuneiform (from the Latin word for 'wedge-shaped'). It represented sounds as well as objects. This way of writing was used for 3,000 years.

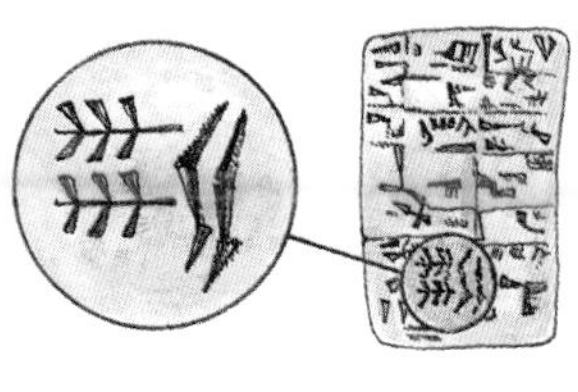

The earliest writing

Sumerian pictograms
5,500 years ago

Egyptian hieroglyphs
5,000 years ago

Cuneiform 4,800 years ago

Writing in the Indus Valley
4,600 years ago

Writing in Crete
4,000 years ago

Writing in China
3,500 years ago

Prehistoric survivors

Over millions of years, plants and animals evolve: they adapt to the world around them. Ancestors of the horse, for example, had toes instead of hoofs and were the size of cats.

Equus (horse) 2 m.y.a.

Hyracotherium 55 m.y.a.

Living fossils

A few plants and animals have not evolved since prehistoric times. They are called 'living fossils'. Some of the most well-known are listed here.

Gingko (tree)

Living gingko trees have survived almost unchanged for the last 195 million years. They were growing when dinosaurs lived on Earth.

Metasequoia (tree)

This pine tree, also called the Dawn Redwood, grew on Earth 100 m.y.a. Unlike other pine trees, it loses its leaves in winter.

Australian lungfish

This fish, discovered in Australia in 1869, has a fossil record that goes back 225 million years.

Limulus (sea animal)

Limulus first lived on Earth 170 m.y.a. Though rare, they can be found today along the Atlantic coast of the USA. They are related to the giant water scorpions that lived 500 m.y.a.

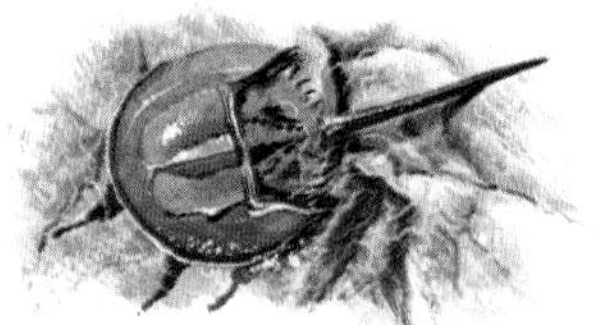

Nautilus (sea animal)

Many nautiluses lived in the seas between 230 and 65 m.y.a. One type, that lived 22 m.y.a., can still be found in the Indian Ocean.

Lingula (sea animal)

This lampshell has one of the longest fossil records of any animal – 570 million years.

Tuatara (reptile)

Living on islands off New Zealand, this rare lizard's ancestors lived 200 m.y.a.

Duck-billed platypus

This sea mammal, found in Australia in 1797, has a fossil record of at least 150 million years.

Okapi (mammal)

Okapis were discovered living in Africa in 1900. They have existed since 30 m.y.a.

Peripatus (worm)

This worm lives in the tropical jungle. Its ancestor lived 500 m.y.a. on the sea-floor.

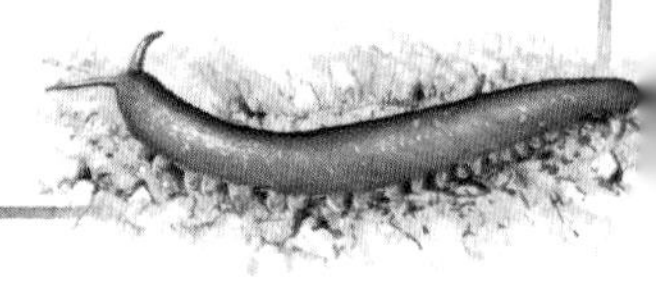

The most famous living fossil is the coelacanth. This fish was thought to have become extinct 65 m.y.a. Then, one was caught alive by fishermen off the coast of South Africa in 1938. It was 1.5m long (5ft) and weighed 58kg (128lb).

It was later found that the fishermen of Madagascar caught these fish quite often. They used the coarse, scaly skin to roughen the inner tubes of bicycle tyres, when mending a puncture.

The Loch Ness Monster

There have been many reports of people claiming to see a huge creature in Loch Ness in Scotland ('loch' is a Gaelic word for 'lake'). The loch is very deep and was linked in prehistoric times to the North Sea. Some people believe that these monsters (if they exist) may be prehistoric animals trapped in the loch, and that they may be Elasmosaurs (a type of Plesiosaur) that lived 60 m.y.a.

There are about 12 Scottish lakes, apart from Loch Ness, where people claim to have seen monsters. And similar monsters have been reported swimming in fresh water lakes all over the world.

Name	Location
Slimey Slim	USA
Manipogo	Canada
Pooka	Ireland
Piast	Ireland
Waitoreke	Australia
Hvaler Serpent	Norway
Storsjö	Sweden
White Lake Monster	Chile

Common living fossils

Living fossils are usually thought of as rare. However, there are some that are quite familiar. These are shown in the table on the right.

Name	Species	First on earth
Turtles	Reptile	275 m.y.a.
Crocodiles	Reptile	195
Silverfish	Insect	395
Cockroaches	Insect	345
Monkey puzzle	Tree	250
Magnolia	Tree	140

Prehistoric words

Naming the periods of Earth's history

Cambrian (570-500 m.y.a.)

Cambria is Latin for Wales, where rocks of this age were first studied.

Ordovician (500-435 m.y.a.)

The Ordovices were a tribe who once lived in Wales, where Ordovician rocks were first studied.

Silurian 435-395 m.y.a.

The Silures were an ancient Welsh tribe who lived in the area where Silurian rocks were first studied.

Devonian (395-345 m.y.a.)

This period is named after Devon, a county in southern England.

Carboniferous (345-280 m.y.a.)

This period is named after carbon (carbo = 'coal' in Latin) because coal was formed in this period.

Permian (280-230 m.y.a.)

This period is named after the Perm district in the Russian Ural mountains.

Triassic (230-195 m.y.a.)

Named after the fact that rocks of this period in Germany are divided into 3 distinct layers (treis = 'three' in Greek)

Jurassic (195-141 m.y.a.)

Named after the Jura mountains in France.

Cretaceous (141-65 m.y.a.)

'Creta' is Latin for chalk, which is common in Cretaceous rocks.

Tertiary (65-2 m.y.a.)
Quarternary (2 m.y.a. to present)

Geologists once divided rocks into 4 groups: Primary, Secondary, Tertiary, Quarternary. Primary and Secondary are no longer used.

The Tertiary is divided into 5 epochs:

Palaeocene	65-55 m.y.a.
Eocene	55-38 m.y.a.
Oligocene	38-22 m.y.a.
Miocene	22-6 m.y.a.
Pliocene	6-2 m.y.a.

The Quarternary is divided into 2 epochs:
Pleistocene 2 m.y.a. to 10,000 years ago
Holocene (Recent) 10,000 years ago to present.

Studying prehistory

Someone who studies the fossil remains of plants, animals, and human beings is called a **palaeontologist**. (palaios = 'old' in Greek)

Someone who studies the Earth's rocks and soil is called a **geologist**. (ge = 'Earth' in Greek)

Someone who studies human evolution, customs, and societies is called an **anthropologist**. (anthropos = 'human being' in Greek)

Someone who studies the remains of buildings, burial grounds, and the objects made by early human beings and ancient civilisations is called an **archaeologist**, (arkhaiologia = 'study of ancient history' in Greek)

Index

First published in 1986. Usborne Publishing Ltd, Usborne House, 83-85 Saffron Hill, London EC1N 8RT.